D1016911

DRACULA

The Young Collector's
Illustrated Classics

By
Bram Stoker

Adapted by
Leigh Hope Wood

Illustrated by
Ned Butterfield

Cover Art by
Ned Butterfield

A Division of Kidsbooks, Inc.
3535 West Peterson Avenue
Chicago, IL 60659

Manufactured in the United States of America

Contents

Introduction
The Mystery of Count Dracula 9

PART ONE
Visiting Dracula's Castle

Chapter 1
A Strange Journey 13

Chapter 2
To The Castle 19

Chapter 3
The Count .29

Chapter 4
A Prisoner .39

PART TWO
Friends in England

Chapter 5
Mina Visits Lucy 55

Chapter 6
The Ghost Ship 67

Chapter 7
Lucy's Sleepwalking 77

Chapter 8
Dr. Seward's Bizarre Patient 85

PART THREE
Lucy Finds Peace

Chapter 9
A Change for the Worse 93

Chapter 10
The Wolf 107

Chapter 11
Van Helsing's Mission 115

Chapter 12
Lucy's Tomb 125

PART FOUR
Hunting Down Count Dracula

Chapter 13
Gathering Evidence 139

Chapter 14
Looking for Clues 149

Chapter 15
Encounters with the Count 159

Chapter 16
The Final Struggle 177

Introduction:

The Mystery of Count Dracula

In the tale you are about to read, many strange things begin happening in England, and no one can figure out why! No one suspects that evil lurks about. If not for the diaries, newspaper clippings, and letters kept by the people caught in the middle of this terror, Count Dracula would go unsuspected by all.

It all begins with young Jonathan Harker. He is the first to experience Dracula's power. The diary that he keeps records the Count's dark deeds in the Castle Dracula. Likewise, it is his beloved, Mina Murray, who records the strange events occurring in England. Unknown to her, these happenings are brought about by Dracula's arrival from Transylvania.

It is only when Mina's friend, Lucy Westenra, falls ill to an unexplainable disease, that the mystery begins to unravel. Dr. Van Helsing, a famous scientist and physician from Amsterdam, is called by a friend of the family. He thinks he knows what is happening, but will others believe him?

Evidence must be collected, and when Van Helsing has proof, he can organize the hunt for Count Dracula!

Part One

VISITING DRACULA'S CASTLE

Chapter

A STRANGE JOURNEY

Jonathan Harker's Diary
May 3

I am now well on my way to meet Count Dracula. I left Munich in the evening on May 1, and arrived in Vienna early the next morning. Before my connecting train left, I took a little walk through the city. I felt then that I was surely leaving the West and entering the East, to a place with different customs, influenced by Turkish rule.

My next train left on time and brought me to Klausenburgh, where I stayed for the night. I found that my knowledge of German would be very helpful. I thought to myself that perhaps I was more prepared for this trip than I had imagined.

While in London, I had investigated as much as I could, searching among books and maps for information on Transylvania. Since I would be dealing with a nobleman of that country, I wanted to know as much as I could of the land and its people.

I was not able to find a map that provided the exact location of Castle Dracula, but I did find other pieces of information. Bistritz, the place I am headed, is in the midst of the Carpathian Mountains. The people I will be among claim to be descended from Attila and the Huns. Supposedly, every superstition in the world is gathered here. I must ask the Count about all of them.

The night I spent in Klausenburgh, I did not sleep well because there was a dog howling all night under my window. Then,

the next morning I had to hurry through breakfast to catch my train. All day the train moved across the land, making one stop after another. I saw little towns and castles at the top of steep hills, and rivers, swept clear on their banks by flood.

It was dark before I reached Bistritz. Count Dracula had directed me to go to the Golden Krone Hotel. I was evidently expected there, for I was met at the door by a cheerful, old peasant woman who knew my name. So it was here that I spent the night.

May 4

I found that Count Dracula had directed my landlord to reserve the best place on the coach for me. Although I asked many questions of my landlord regarding Count Dracula, he acted as if he could not understand my German. This could not be true, because up to then he had understood it very well.

Just before I left, the landlord's wife came to my room in an excited state and asked if I really needed to go to Castle Dracula. I told her I needed to go at once, for I was engaged in important business.

"But it is a very bad day for it," she said. "It is the eve of St. George's Day. When the clock strikes midnight, all the evil things in the world will come out. Do you know where you are going?"

I assured her I had to go. She then

took a crucifix from her neck and put it around my own. I am not feeling very good about this trip now. If this book should ever reach my sweet Mina before I do, let it bring her my goodbye. Here comes the coach!

Chapter

TO THE CASTLE

May 5

There are many odd things to write about concerning my trip in the coach and my arrival at Castle Dracula. First, when the coach arrived, my landlady had a few words with the driver. Overhearing what she said, I took out my dictionary and translated the meaning of her words. She said something about Satan, hell, and vampires.

When we started, the crowd around the inn all made the sign of the cross and

pointed two fingers toward me. I asked a fellow passenger what this meant. He said it was a charm against the evil eye.

This whole business at the inn made me even more uneasy about my trip. But, after we got on our way, I lost myself in the countryside. There were forests and sloping green hills, all overshadowed by the great Carpathians. Right and left, the mountains towered, with the falling sun bringing out all their beautiful colors.

The driver was in great haste to get to the place where I would be dropped off and met by Count Dracula's coach. We were flying over the rugged road. When it grew dark, the passengers seemed to be urging him to go even faster.

We soon came to the place where the other coach should have been waiting. We were early, but the driver wanted to proceed and not wait for Dracula's coach. The other passengers seemed relieved, but I was greatly disappointed. I did not want to make the trip again.

Then, our horses began to neigh and snort, and a coach drew up.

"You are early tonight, my friend," Dracula's driver said to ours.

"The Englishman was in a hurry," our driver replied.

"And *you* wished him to go on without being met by Dracula's coach. You cannot deceive me. I know too much, and my horses are swift."

The strange driver had very red lips and sharp-looking teeth, as white as ivory.

"Give me his bags," he said.

Soon my bags were in the coach, and I was pulled up by the hand of this strange man, who had a grip of steel. Then, we were on our way at a great pace.

After a while, I realized that we were going in circles and became concerned about the time. I struck a match and discovered it was almost midnight. Nearby, a dog began to howl and then another. Soon the air was full of this wailing.

We were climbing and descending, but mostly climbing. Suddenly, I became aware of the driver pulling the horses into the courtyard of a ruined castle, whose battlements showed a jagged line against the moonlit sky. Not one ray of light came from the tall windows.

The driver helped me down, and again I noticed his strong grip. I was left with my bags at a great door, old and studded with large iron nails. The driver got back up on his coach and took the horses under one of the dark archways surrounding the courtyard.

I stood in silence for awhile, thinking how I came to be in such a strange place. This was my last job as a lawyer's clerk. Now I am a full-blown lawyer, I thought to myself, for I had just received word before leaving London that I had passed my exam.

Just then, I heard the approach of footsteps and heard the creaking of the door. I was met by a tall old man with a long mustache who was dressed in black. He motioned to me.

"Welcome to my house! Enter freely and of your own will!"

The instant I entered, he grabbed my hand. His hand was as cold as ice, like the hand of a dead man, but his grip

was strong, like that of the driver.

"Count Dracula?" I asked.

"I am Dracula," he replied, as he bowed in a courtly way. "I bid you welcome, Mr. Harker. You must need to eat and rest. It is late, and my people are not available. Let me see to your comfort myself."

He took my luggage and led me down a dark hallway to another heavy door. When he threw this open, I saw a well-lit room in which a fire had been made and a table set for supper. Through this room he led me to another, where there was a great bed and another fireplace. The Count left the luggage and withdrew.

"After you freshen up, join me in the other room, where you will find supper prepared."

Now feeling more at ease, I realized that I was half starving. Hastily, I made myself ready for dinner and went to the other room. My supper was laid out already, and my host stood by the fireplace.

"Please, be seated," he said. "You will,

I trust, excuse me. I have dined already."

I ate my dinner with enthusiasm and then joined the Count by the fire. While we talked, I noticed his hands. They had at first seemed very fine and white. Looking more closely, I noticed they were broad and coarse, with hair growing from the center of the palm and long nails cut at a sharp point. Once, when he leaned over and touched me, a horrible feeling of nausea overcame me. It may have been because his breath smelled so bitter and sweet, like the odor of blood.

Not long after, I saw the first dim streak of the coming dawn and heard the howling of wolves down in the valley below. The Count's eyes gleamed.

"Listen to them—the children of the night. What music they make!"

I suppose my expression grew strange, for he began to explain himself.

"Ah, sir, you people in the city cannot understand the feelings of the hunter." Then he rose.

"You must be tired," he said. "You may sleep as long as you like. I have to be away until the late afternoon. So, sweet dreams."

He then left me to myself, and I went to bed.

Chapter

THE COUNT

May 7

I slept most of the day and awoke to find breakfast already laid out for me. I ate and then began to investigate my surroundings. I found that the decorations in my rooms were several centuries old, but in good condition. What seemed odd, though, was that there was no bell to ring for servants and not one mirror in any of the rooms. I had to use a small glass I carry when traveling in order to shave.

I didn't want to go about the castle

without the Count's permission, but I did venture to open one door leading from my room and found a small library. While I was looking at the books there, the Count entered.

"I'm glad you have found your way here," he said. "These books are good companions. Ever since I had the idea to go to your London, I have come here to learn about England. Although I only know the language through books, I hope that you will help me to speak it better."

"But, Count," I replied, "you speak the language very well."

"Thank you for your flattery," he said. "True, I know the grammar and the words, but I do not know how to speak it. As long as you are here to tell me about my new estate in London, you may as well remain here with me awhile. In this way, I will learn how to speak to the people of England."

I could only do as he wished, for he was the client of my employer, Peter Hawkins. I asked if I might come to this library often while remaining as his guest.

"You may go anywhere you like," he replied, "except where the doors are locked, where you will certainly not wish to go."

We then began talking of Transylvania and London. He also wanted to know more about his new estate and how I had found it. I described the place to him.

"The estate contains some twenty acres and is surrounded by a great stone wall. The house must date back to medieval times. It has very few windows, and they are high up and heavily barred with iron. It also has an old chapel and church. There are very few houses close by. There is a very large house that has recently been converted into an insane asylum, but it is not visible from your estate."

"I am glad it is old and big. I myself am from a very old family. To live in a new house would kill me."

We went over the deed, and I got his signature on some of the papers and wrote to Mr. Hawkins. Not long after this, the Count left for awhile. I occupied myself with the books around me. There was an atlas opened to a map of London. On it, the Count had circled the place where his new estate was situated. There were two other circles at Exeter and Whitby.

When the Count returned, he led me from the library and I found, to my surprise, that the table had been set for supper. Because he had dined out on his way home, he again sat by as I ate. After dinner we talked until dawn, then he abruptly jumped up and said he should be going.

May 8

This place is so strange that I'm beginning to wish I had never come. I have only the Count to speak with, and I fear I am the only living soul in the place. Let me explain.

I only slept a few hours after the Count left, and feeling I could not go back to sleep, I got up. I had just hung my shaving glass by the window and was beginning to shave when I felt a hand on my shoulder.

"Good morning," the Count said.

I jumped and cut myself slightly, for it amazed me that he was behind me but I hadn't seen him in my mirror. I looked again to be sure. And it was true. His reflection was not there.

When I turned to greet the Count, he caught sight of the blood on my chin. His eyes blazed and suddenly he made a grab for my throat. I drew away, and his hand touched the crucifix I had been given by my landlady at the inn in Bistritz. His fury seemed to pass as quickly as it had come.

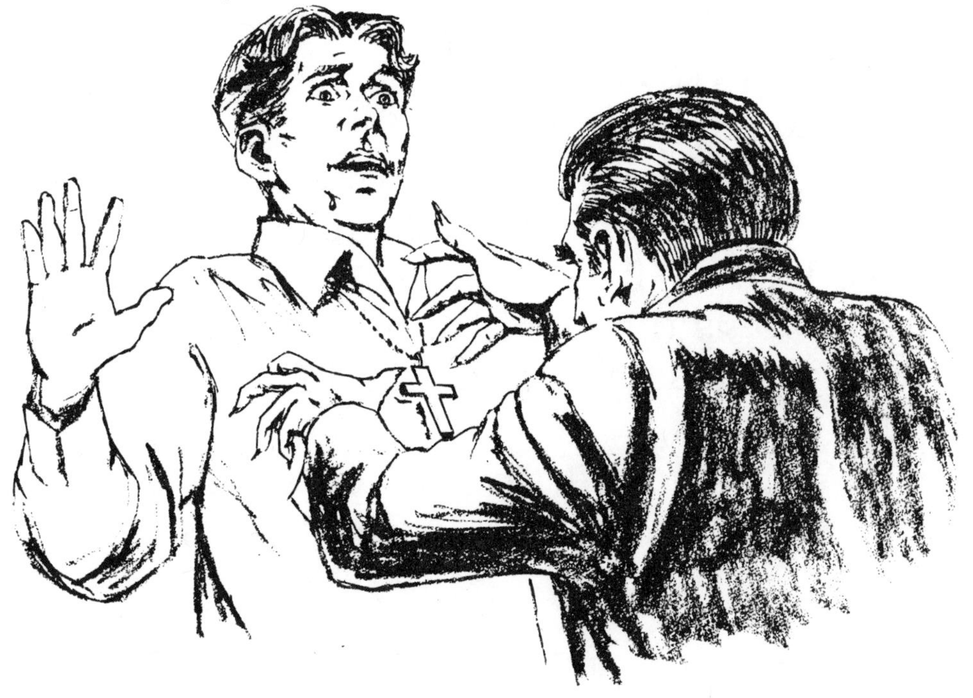

"Take care," he said. "Take care how you cut yourself. It is more dangerous than you think in this country. And this is the thing that had done the mischief."

He picked up my shaving mirror and tossed it out the window. He then left without another word.

I again had breakfast alone and began to think that the Count was a very peculiar man. I had never seen him eat or drink! After breakfast, I went into another room that had a view of the south. On that side, the castle sits on the very edge of a cliff. A stone falling from the window would travel a thousand feet before hitting the ground.

When I had seen the view, I explored further and found that all the other doors were locked. In no place, except for the windows, is there an exit for me. The castle is as good as a prison, and I am a prisoner!

Once I found this out, a wild feeling came over me. I rushed up and down the

stairs, trying every door and peering out every window I could find. Then, the feeling that I was helpless overpowered me, and I sat down quietly to think.

I am still thinking about what is the best thing for me to do. The Count cannot be trusted. That is certain, for he is the one who has imprisoned me. But I will not let on that I know.

Chapter

A PRISONER

May 12

The Count and I have had several talks. After one such discussion on legal matters in England, he asked me if I had written Mr. Hawkins again. I answered that I hadn't (for of course I had seen no way of getting a letter out of the castle).

"Write now, my young friend," Count Dracula said. "Write to him and to any other, and say that you shall stay with me until a month from now."

"You wish me to stay so long?" I asked.

"I do," he replied.

I bowed, for I knew that I was a prisoner.

"I hope, my young friend, that you will not talk of things other than business in your letters. Just say that you are well and that you look forward to getting home soon."

As he spoke, he handed me three sheets of paper and three envelopes. They were all made of the thinnest paper, and I knew he would be able to see what I wrote. I decided to write very formal letters to Mr. Hawkins and to Mina in order to cause suspicion at home.

When I was through, the Count took my letters and departed. But before leaving, he gave me a warning.

"I have work to do this evening, my young friend. I hope you will find things as you wish. Let me advise you not to leave these rooms. If you do, and you feel that you may fall asleep, you should hasten back to your room. You should not be caught sleeping anywhere else, for only here is it safe."

When the Count left me, I went to my room. But after awhile, not hearing any sound, I went to the other room, where I could look out towards the south. As I leaned out the window, trying to drink in the beauty of the landscape and clear my head, I saw something moving below me. I drew back and carefully looked out.

From a window below, the Count's head appeared. Slowly, he emerged and began to crawl down the castle wall, face down with his cloak spreading over him like wings. I saw his fingers

grasp the corners of the stone, as he moved with great speed down the stone wall, like a lizard.

May 15

Once more I have seen the Count go down the castle wall in his lizard fashion. As soon as he was gone, I went about trying to find a way out. I managed to get to the door where I had entered the castle, but it was locked on the inside and there was no key to this lock.

I went on to examine other rooms and found one where the door was off its hinges. It was evidently part of the castle occupied by ladies in bygone days. Although dusty, it seemed more comfortable. I found that a soft quiet came over me. I sat down at a small writing table and entered the day's events in my diary.

When I finished, I put my book and pen in my pocket. I felt sleepy then and took pleasure in disobeying the Count's warning. I pulled a great couch into the moonlight and lay down for the night.

It seemed that I was not alone. In the moonlight opposite me were three young women. I thought I was dreaming. Although the moonlight was behind them, they threw no shadow. They came close to me, whispered to each other, and then laughed.

One of the ladies came toward me and licked her lips like an animal. She was about to fasten her teeth on my throat, when she was pulled back by the Count. He was furious. His eyes were blazing red. With a sweep of his arms, he hurled the woman away.

"How dare you touch him. This man belongs to me!"

I must have fainted here, or it was all a dream. But I don't think it was a dream. I awoke in my own bed, but my clothes were not laid out as usual. Also, it is my habit to wind my watch before going to bed, and it was unwound.

If not a dream, then that night has

shown me the trouble I'm in. My room is certainly a sanctuary, from those awful women at least, who are waiting to suck my blood.

May 19

I am surely in trouble. Last night the Count asked me to write three letters, one saying that my work was nearly done, the second saying that I should start for home soon, and the last saying that I was starting out the next morning. He reasoned that I should do so because the postal service was so bad. I acted as if I agreed and asked how I should date the letters.

"The first should be June 12, the second June 19, and the third June 29," he answered.

Now I know how long I have to live!

June 17

Today, as I sat on my bed with my head in my hands, awaiting my death, I heard the cracking of whips and the pounding of horses' feet. I hurried to the window and saw two large wagons come into the courtyard. They were driven by gypsies. I cried to them for help, but they only looked up and pointed at me and laughed.

The wagons contained great boxes with handles of thick rope. The boxes must have been empty, for the gypsies carried them with ease. They unloaded them and disappeared within the castle.

June 29

The gypsies have been working in the castle for some time now, everyday carting great boxes up the hill. I have heard spades and hammers. Something is going on, and my time is drawing near. I must act!

It has always been at night that the Count has come to my room, and I have never been threatened during the day by the strange, blood-sucking women. Can it be that he and the women sleep when others are awake, and that they are awake while we sleep?

The only way to get to him during the day is through his window. Why shouldn't I do as the Count does and try to scale the wall? It is risky, but I have no choice. I may fall a thousand feet to my death, or find some clue that may lead to freedom. If I fail, goodbye Mina!

Same day, later —

I did it, and I've made it back to my

room! I went while my courage was up. Climbing down the wall to the Count's window was not so frightening as entering the Count's room. Luckily, he was not there. The only thing I found there was a pile of gold. In the corner, however, was a great wooden door. I tried it, and much to my surprise it was open.

The door led down a passageway to

steep stairs and another hallway. Here was the odor of old earth newly turned. As I continued down the passage, the odor became stronger. At last, I pulled open another heavy door and found that I was in a chapel.

The boxes brought by the gypsies were here, and they were now filled with earth. I tried to find a passageway leading out of the castle, but there was none. I then went down into the vaults, hoping to make some discovery—and I did. In one of the great boxes, on a pile of dirt, lay the Count!

The Count looked neither dead nor alive. His eyes were glassy, but his lips were as red as ever. I searched him for the keys to the front door, but I found none. Then, I quickly fled from the chapel and made it back to my room.

June 30

This morning I have decided to take my life into my own hands. Yesterday was the date of my last letter posted by the Count, and today I watched the gypsies take all the big boxes away. So, I am alone in the castle with those awful

women, but I will not remain.

I have decided to scale the castle wall. I will take some of the Count's gold. If I make it down the wall, maybe the gold can get me away from this place and back to London. If I fall, then at least I will save myself from the blood-sucking women. Goodbye, all! Goodbye, Mina!

Part Two

FRIENDS IN ENGLAND

Chapter

MINA VISITS LUCY

Letter from Mina Murray to Lucy Westenra

May 9

My Dearest Lucy,

Forgive my long delay in writing. The life of an assistant schoolmistress is sometimes hard. I long to be with my good friend by the sea, so we can talk of our future lives. I have been trying to keep up with Jonathan's studies. I am learning shorthand and typing so that I can help him with his work. We are both keeping a journal in shorthand. Did I tell you that he passed his exam? He is a lawyer now, or will be as soon as he returns from Transylvania.

I just received a note from Jonathan. He is well, and will be returning in about a week. I wonder if he and I will see strange countries together after we're married. Well, I must be going. Tell me all the news when you write. I hear rumors, especially of a tall, handsome, curly-haired man???

Your loving Mina

Letter from Lucy Westenra to Mina Murray

Wednesday

My Dearest Mina,

There is very little to tell. As to the tall, curly-haired man, I suppose it is Mr. Arthur Holmwood. He often comes to see us. He and mamma get on very well. Some time ago he introduced us to a man who would suit you very well, if you weren't engaged to Jonathan. He is a young doctor who has in his care a whole lunatic asylum. He is very calm but very determined, and has a way of looking one right in the eye. He must have real power over his patients.

Oh, Mina, we have told each other our secrets all our lives. Oh, can't you guess about the curly-haired man? I think he loves me. I love him, my dear Arthur. I do want to tell you all. I must stop for now. Remember that this is a secret. Write to me soon.

Lucy

Letter from Lucy Westenra to Mina Murray

May 24

My Dearest Mina,

Thanks for your sweet letter. It was so nice to be able to tell you about Arthur. But when it rains it pours. Just today I have had three proposals of marriage!

Number One came just before lunch. I told you about him. His name is Dr. John Seward, the lunatic-asylum man. He was very sweet, but I'm afraid I had to tell him I was in love with another. He then stood up and looked very strong and serious. He took my hands and vowed to be my friend forever. Then he left, and I felt horrible!

Number Two came after lunch. He is such a nice fellow, an American from Texas. He has had many adventures. His name is Quincey P. Morris. When he came in, he found me alone and asked if I would want to "hitch up alongside him" and "go down the road in a double harness." I had to giggle, but then he got very serious and asked for my hand in a more formal way. Again, I had to tell the truth, that I was in love with another. Like Dr. Seward, this good Mr. Morris answered me by vowing to be my friend.

Of course, you know who Number Three is. I don't know what I have done to deserve him, my Arthur, friend and husband. Goodbye, dear Mina. I hope we will see each other soon.

Lucy

Mina Murray's Diary
July 24

Lucy met me at the station in Whitby, looking sweeter than ever. I am so happy to see my friend at last! We rode about the town, which is very lovely. There is a church, around which is a large graveyard. This spot is perhaps the nicest in all the town, for it looks out on the harbor. There are walks, with benches along the way. People go and sit there all day. I shall go there as often as I can.

July 25

I brought Lucy to my favorite spot up on the cliff overlooking the harbor. We sat on the bench there, and she told me about Arthur. It made me a little heart-sick for Jonathan, for I haven't heard from him for a whole week.

I returned to my bench later in the day alone. I am very sad. Again, there was no letter from Jonathan.

July 26

I have had no news from Jonathan for quite some time. Luckily, Mr. Hawkins sent me a letter from him, because I had written to him to see if he had heard anything. It is a strange letter, only one-line long that says he is starting for home. This formal style is not like Jonathan. It makes me uneasy.

Also, there is Lucy. Although she is well, she's taken to her old habit of sleep-walking. I must lock our door at night to keep her from wandering off in her night clothes!

August 6

I have still not heard from Jonathan, and Lucy is more excitable than ever. She has not walked much in her sleep in the last week, but she seems to watch me at night. She tries the door, and finding it locked, goes about the room searching for the key.

Today, everything is gray. The fisher-men say we're in for a terrible storm. All the boats are racing for home. When I was on my bench watching the mist roll in from the sea, the coastguard approached. He had his spyglass under his arm. He stopped to talk but was all the time looking out to sea at a strange ship.

"I can't make her out," he said.

"She's a Russian ship, by the look of her, but she's knocking about in the strangest way. She can't decide which direction to take, as if she's not minding the hand on the wheel. We'll hear more of her before this time tomorrow."

Chapter

THE GHOST SHIP

Cutting from "The Dailygraph" Newspaper
August 8, Whitby
(pasted in Mina Murray's Diary)

One of the greatest and most sudden storms on record has been experienced here at Whitby. The weather has not been too uncommon for the month of August, and Saturday afternoon was mild. But in the evening, the wind fell away, and by midnight there was calm. All the boats had come in but one. She was a foreign schooner with all sails set. Signals were sent to her to reduce sails in face of her danger.

A little after midnight, a strange sound came over the sea. At once the waves rose in growing fury. All calm was lost, as the wind roared like thunder. It was hard to keep one's footing on the pier, so everyone was cleared off. Suddenly, from a higher vantage point, on top of the cliff, we could see masses of sea fog rolling in.

The spotlight was set on the harbor and beyond, and once, when the fog cleared for a moment, we could see the schooner heading for the harbor. She rushed across the harbor and pitched herself on the sand and gravel washed in by many tides.

The very instant the shore was touched, an immense dog sprang from the deck and ran forward, then jumped from the bow onto the sand. It ran toward the cliff and disappeared into the dark-

ness. Curiously, the sea calmed and the storm passed.

All the people who had been watching up on the cliff, took off down the steps that lead to the pier. By the time I got to the derelict ship, a crowd had gathered. By the courtesy of the chief boatman, I was allowed on board with other authorities.

At the steering wheel of the boat was a dead sailor. His hands were tied to the wheel with rope and a string of beads, on which hung a crucifix. In the man's pocket was a bottle, carefully corked and containing a little roll of paper.

"The Dailygraph," August 9, Whitby

Much has been learned about the derelict ship that landed here. It is a Russian schooner that came from Varna and is called the Demeter. Her cargo consists solely of a number of great wooden boxes, which have been claimed by a lawyer here in Whitby. The dog that was seen jumping off board has not been found.

Of great interest is the paper found in the pocket of the sailor, who, as it turns out, was the captain of the ship. With the help of a Russian translator, and by permission of the authorities, I am able to reveal some of the paper's contents. Here is part of the captain's account:

> Such strange things are happening, that I shall try to keep an accurate record.
>
> On July 14—I noted something about the crew. They were anxious. They said there was something on board, and crossed themselves.

On July 16—the first mate reported in the morning that one of the crew was missing. Men are more downcast than ever. They said they had expected something of the kind, but they would not say more, just that there was something on board.

On July 17—one of the men came to me and said he thought there was a strange man on board. He said he saw this man while on watch last night. He was in a panic, so I decided to search the ship. We searched from corner to corner, and there were only the great boxes.

July 22—We've had rough weather for the last three days. We've had no time to be frightened.

July 24—Last night another man was lost. Like the first, he came off his watch and was never seen again. There seems some doom over this ship.

July 29—Another tragedy. Second mate was lost last night.

July 30—We are nearing England. Weather is fine, and all sails are set. But I found, after sleeping soundly for first time in awhile, that we've lost two more men. There is only myself, first mate, and two hands left to work the ship.

August 1—We've had two days of fog. I had hoped to be able to signal for help as soon as we reached the English Channel, but I have sighted no other sails. Now so short of hands, we cannot work our sails. I dare not lower them, as we could not raise them again.

August 2—Hearing a cry, I woke up after a few minutes of sleep. I rushed on deck and ran into my first mate. The man on watch is gone.

August 3—At midnight I went to relieve the man at the wheel, but when I got to it there was no one there. I dared not leave the wheel, so I shouted for my first mate. He came up in a panic. He said, "I saw it, like a man, tall and thin, and ghastly pale. I am going to look for it in the boxes."

He went below, and I waited at the wheel. Just as I was beginning to hope that the mate would come out calmer, there came a startled scream that made my blood run cold. He came running up on board, and, before I could say a thing, he jumped into the sea.

August 4—All night I stayed at the wheel, and in the dimness of the night, I saw him. The first mate was right to jump into the sea, but I am captain and must stay on board. I will baffle this monster by tying

myself to the wheel with my crucifix and beads. I shall at least save my soul. Maybe this bottle will be found in my pocket, so that others will know what became of the *Demeter*.

Chapter

LUCY'S SLEEPWALKING

Mina Murray's Diary
August 11—3 AM

There is no sleep for me now. Lucy and I have had such an adventure, an awful experience really. I fell asleep as soon as I closed my journal. Suddenly, I became fully awake, and sat up, with a horrible sense of fear. Lucy's bed was empty! I had forgotten to lock the bedroom door!

I ran downstairs. She wasn't anywhere to be found. Then, I came to the

hall door and found it open. I took a heavy shawl and ran out in my night clothes, as Lucy must have done. When I came to the great cliff, I looked across the way, toward the churchyard, for a white figure. I hoped she had found her way to our favorite bench.

There was a bright moon, which was covered every now and then by clouds. For a moment I could see nothing, but

then as the moon came out from the clouds, I saw Lucy. She was lying on a bench, and a dark figure stood over her.

I ran all the way to the churchyard. As I approached, I called out to her. Something raised a head. It seemed to be a white face, with red gleaming eyes. Lucy did not answer me, but I continued to call her name.

When I came to the bench, the dark

figure was gone. Lucy was still asleep and was breathing with difficulty. As I came closer, she put her hand to her throat and shuddered. I threw my shawl around her and fastened it at the neck with a pin. I then put my shoes on her feet and began to wake her as gently as I could.

Lucy awoke and seemed not to know where she was. I told her to come with me at once, and she obeyed. I led her along the stone paths, which made me wince all the way, as my feet were now bare. Luckily, we got home without anyone noticing us. We vowed not to tell anyone.

Same day, noon—

All goes well. Lucy slept well, and her health apparently did not suffer from her night in the cold air. In fact, she is quite rosy. However, I was surely very clumsy last night. I must have pricked her with my pin. She has two little holes on her throat, and there is a drop of blood on her nightdress. Luckily, the holes are so small, they probably will not leave a scar.

August 13—

In the middle of the night, I awoke and found Lucy awake. She was sitting in her bed pointing at the window. I got up and drew back the curtain. Against the

moonlight, I could see a large bat coming and going in great circles. It came very close to the window at times but eventually headed out toward the harbor. When I came back to bed, Lucy was asleep.

August 14—

Last night, Lucy went to bed early with a headache. I went out for a little stroll along the cliffs. I was thinking of Jonathan. As I came home, I happened to look up at Lucy's window and saw her head leaning out. She seemed fast asleep. Seated beside her on the sill was what looked like a large bird.

I ran upstairs and came to our room just as she was moving back to her bed. Fast asleep, she was breathing with difficulty and holding her throat. I pulled the covers up around her, then locked the door and closed the window.

Today, Lucy is pale, and there is a tired look about her face. I am afraid that her sleepwalking is beginning to affect her health. However, we had some good news today. Arthur's father, Lord Holmwood, has decided he wants his son's wedding to happen soon. He has been ill for some time. Lucy is happy to marry a little earlier than she thought, and her mother is also.

Poor woman! Today, Lucy's mother told me that her doctor has given her bad news. She has only a few months to live. Her heart is weak, and any sudden shock could kill her. I'm so glad we didn't tell her about Lucy's night on the cliffs!

August 19—

I have been too unhappy to write in my journal, having had no news from Jonathan. Now joy, joy, joy! At last some news! But, not all joy. He has been ill. That is why he has not written. Mr. Hawkins wrote and told me of his illness. Poor Jonathan is in a hospital in Budapest. Mr. Hawkins says it would be a good thing if Jonathan and I were to go ahead and marry. Tomorrow I am taking a train, and I will help nurse him back to health. I am so happy!

Ah, but poor Lucy. She seems to be growing weaker. I do not understand this fading away. She eats and sleeps, but has no energy. At night, I hear her gasping for air. I found her leaning out the window again last night. I suppose she goes there, still asleep, wanting air. When I woke her, she began to cry. I fear that those pin pricks on her neck may be the reason. They are still open and have become larger and white at the edges. I can only hope that her health improves.

Chapter

DR. SEWARD'S BIZARRE PATIENT

Dr. Seward's Diary
August 19

Ever since Lucy turned down my proposal, I have been able to do nothing but work. I eat and sleep little, and work all hours at the asylum. I know I have probably become too focused on one patient in particular, R. M. Renfield. But his case has interested me. Now that he has made a sudden turn, I find that I must go back and review his whole case.

As I have noted, Renfield is confident

and has great physical strength, yet he has periods of gloom. At the end of these periods he always comes back to the same idea—consuming as many lives as possible.

He starts by collecting flies, which he then feeds to spiders. After he has collected spiders, he attracts sparrows to his window and feeds his spiders to them. When he first began this habit, he requested a kitten, to which I suppose he wanted to feed his sparrows. When I would not give in to his request, he ate all the sparrows himself.

All along, Renfield has not shown any sign of violence toward me. He pouts and refuses to talk when he does not get his way, but he has never tried to attack me. In fact, except for his strange habit of consuming lives, he has always been reasonable, not like the other patients here.

Last night, however, there was a sudden change in his behavior. At eight o'clock, he began to get excited and sniff about like a dog. He refused to talk to the attendant.

"You don't count now," he said. "The Master is at hand."

The attendant ran to tell me of this new behavior. I visited Renfield and noted that he seemed to get more and more excited. All at once, a certain mad look came into his eyes. Then he went and sat on the bed and kept quiet. I left his room and told the attendant to keep a close watch on the patient.

At about two o'clock in the morning, the attendant came to wake me. He said that Renfield had escaped. Apparently, the attendant had just checked on him when suddenly he heard the window being pulled out. He ran back to Renfield's room just in time to see the patient's feet going out the window. He ran to the window and saw Renfield run across the grounds and climb over the wall that separates us from an old ruined house.

I told the attendant to get a few more men and meet me outside. We all went over the wall and found the patient pressed against the oak door of the house's chapel. He was talking, as if speaking to someone directly in front of him. I approached with caution, for fear of frightening him. Seeing that he was unaware of my presence, I motioned for the other men to follow.

Just as we approached, I heard him say:

"I am here to do whatever you wish, Master. I await Your commands. I have waited long. I am Your servant. I know You will reward me for my loyalty."

We were able to catch him, but he fought like a tiger. He was in a rage. We now have him in a straightjacket, and he cries of murder.

Part Three

LUCY FINDS PEACE

Chapter

A CHANGE FOR THE WORSE

Lucy Westenra's Diary
Hillingham, August 24

I shall try to write a diary like Mina's. Then, when she returns we can share what we've experienced. I have just received a letter from her, telling me of her marriage to Jonathan. I am happy for her and anxiously await my own wedding day, September 28.

My own health is not good. Today, my throat hurts. Arthur has been here and says that I look well, but in his eyes I saw traces of worry. Last night, I seemed to be dreaming just as I did at Whitby. Perhaps it is the change in air, since we have left our summer place and are now home again. I wonder if I could sleep in mother's room tonight. It is strange how afraid I feel. I keep having those bad dreams, of the bat flying about outside my window.

Letter from Arthur Holmwood to Dr. John Seward

August 31

Dear John,

I want you to do me a favor. Lucy is ill. She has no special disease, but she looks as though she has not an ounce of blood in her. She's ghostly white. I do not dare discuss this with her mother, for the poor woman is herself in a bad state.

I told Lucy that I would ask you to see her. You are to come to lunch at Hillingham tomorrow at two o'clock, so as not to cause suspicion in Mrs. Westenra. We must not let on that Lucy is ill. Unfortunately, I must go see my father, for he too has become worse.

Arthur

Letter from Dr. Seward to Arthur Holmwood

September 2

My dear fellow,

Regarding Miss Westenra's health, I assure you that she has no disease I am aware of. At the same time, I can see how much she has changed. I tested her blood, and it is fine, but she seems to suffer from the lack of it. I also questioned her at length and came to the conclusion that she is suffering from some mental problem.

She told me about her bad dreams and sleepwalking. One night, her friend Miss Mina Murray found her out on a cliff at Whitby. I have written to my good friend, Professor Van Helsing of Amsterdam. He is one of the most advanced scientists of our time. I have great confidence in him.

John Seward

Letter from Dr. Seward
to Arthur Holmwood

September 3

Dear Art,

Van Helsing has come and gone. He agreed with me that Miss Westenra has suffered some blood loss. He said, "There is cause for it, I'm sure." He has gone back home to think. I have been instructed to check on her every day and send word if there is any grave change in her condition. Of course, I will contact you as soon as I have news. I hope your father is improving, dear fellow.

John

Dr. Seward's Diary
September 7

Lucy has taken a turn for the worse. I telegrammed both Arthur and Van Helsing, and have talked to Mrs. Westenra. She seemed more at ease when I told her that the professor would be taking Lucy into his care.

When Van Helsing arrived, he seemed quite troubled. He said, "I have thoughts at present as to what may be at the root of Lucy's trouble. In time, I shall tell you what they are."

We visited Lucy in her room. She looked even worse than the day before. Van Helsing pulled me out of the room.

"We must act quickly. She needs blood or she will die."

"Dr. Van Helsing, I am the strongest.

I shall give my blood to Lucy."

"Get ready then," he said. "I will go down for my bag."

I went downstairs with him, and there in the hallway was Arthur.

"John," he said, "I came at once after receiving your telegram. What can I do? I would give my life to save her."

Van Helsing at once realized who Arthur was.

"Come, dear fellow," Van Helsing said. "We won't ask you to give your life, just your blood."

Arthur was only too willing to give his blood, and the transfusion seemed to do Lucy good. Her cheeks grew more rosy, and her breathing eased.

"You have saved her life," Van Helsing told poor Arthur. "You may give her a kiss but then must be on your way. She needs her rest."

After I saw Arthur to the door, I went back upstairs. Van Helsing was leaning over Lucy. He had her neck exposed.

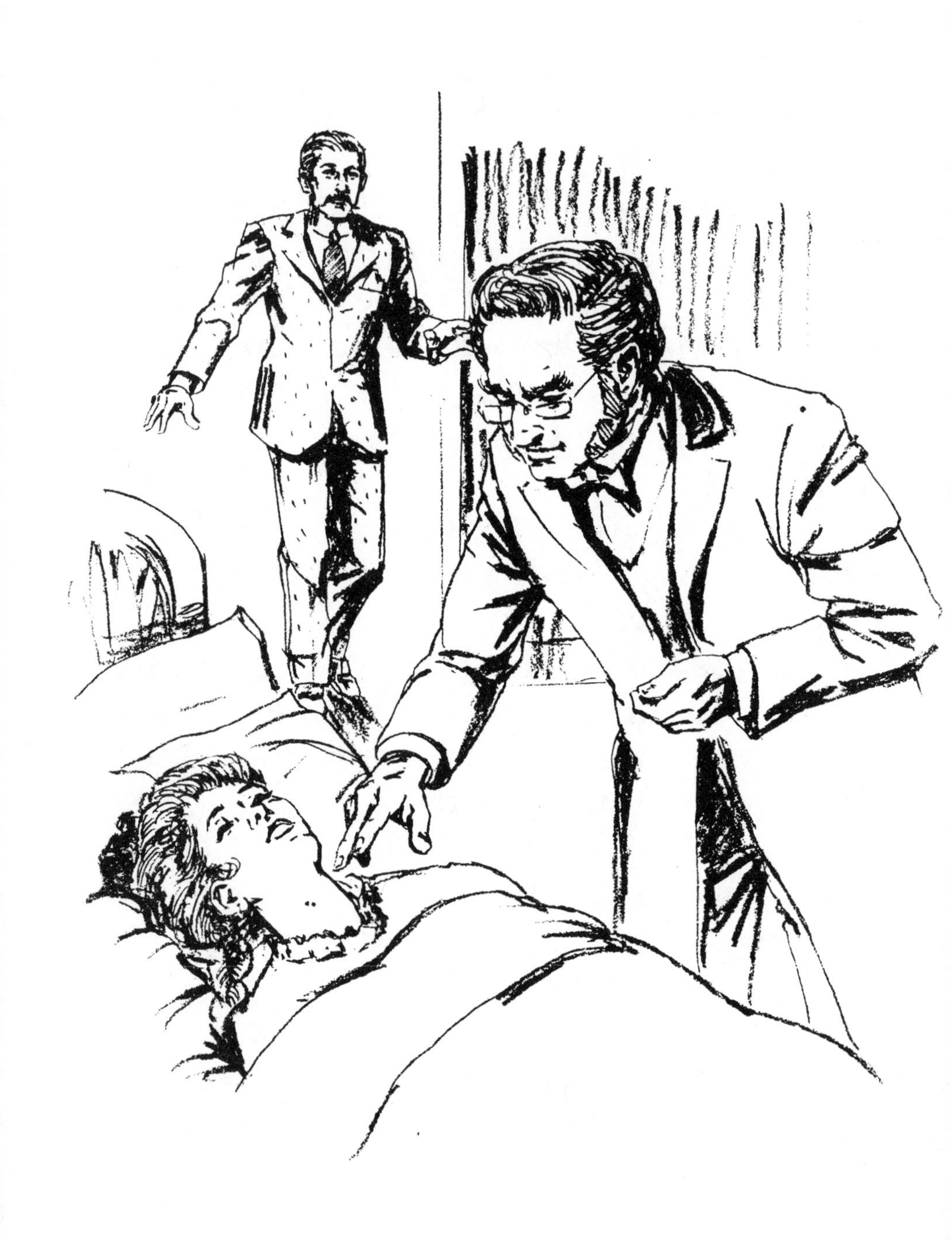

"Come, John. Look at this mark. What do you make of it?" he asked.

"I don't know," I answered.

"I must go back to Amsterdam tonight. There are books and things I shall need. You must stay here tonight and keep your eyes on her at all times. Do not go to sleep and leave her alone."

September 10

I sat up all night with Lucy. She slept soundly and woke at dawn. I returned to my own work, and it was dark before I finished. I received a telegram from Van Helsing, saying I should return to Hillingham that night. He would meet me there the next morning.

I was pretty tired and worn out when I arrived at Hillingham. Lucy was up and in good spirits. She took me by the hands and said, "There will be no sitting up for you tonight. You shall get some sleep. You can sleep in the room next to mine. If there is anything I need, I shall call out to you."

I could not argue with this, for she did seem much improved. After dinner, I lay on the sofa and forgot all about everything. Then, I awoke to Van Helsing's hand on my head. I awoke with a start.

"And how is our patient?"

"When I left her she was quite well."

"Come, let us see," he said.

When we threw open the curtain in Lucy's room, Van Helsing and I were shocked. Lucy lay on the bed whiter than ever. Her lips were pale, and her gums seemed to have shrunken back from the teeth.

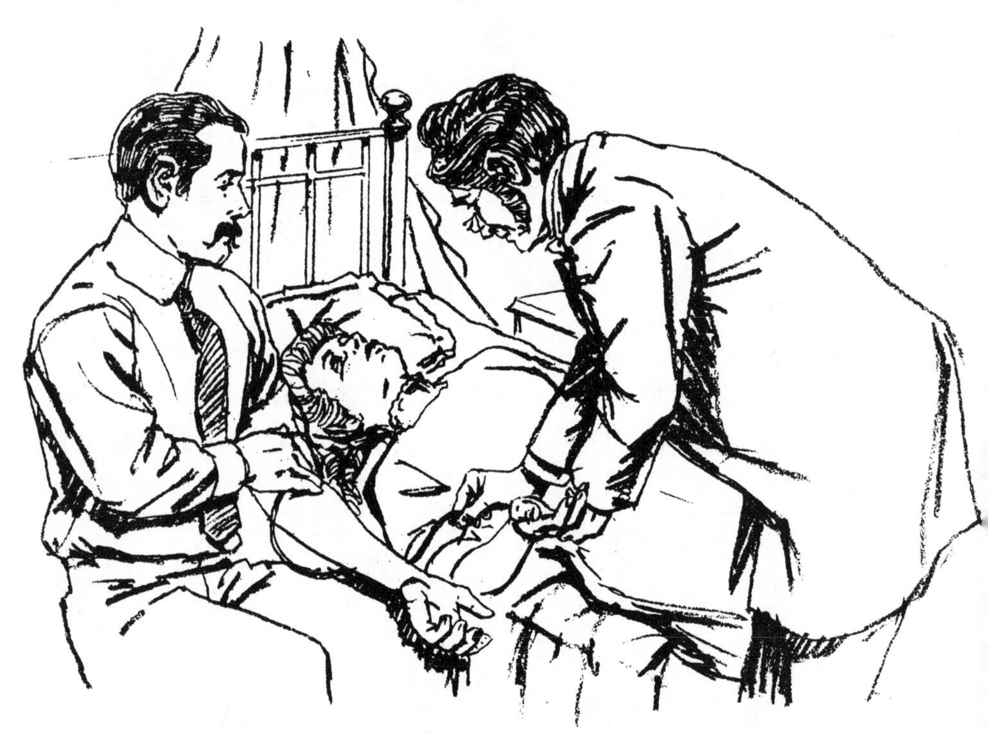

"Quick, John," he said, "we must again give her blood. Roll up your sleeves and get ready."

The transfusion had less of an affect than the last one, but Lucy slept all day and awoke with some energy. In the afternoon, a package arrived from Amsterdam for Van Helsing. It was full of garlic flowers. Van Helsing made a wreath of them and put it around Lucy's neck. He then spread the flowers around her room, especially near the window.

Lucy was not pleased with the smell, but Van Helsing assured her it was for her own good. I, too, thought it was a strange treatment. When we were in the hall, I told him so.

"Professor, you seem to be working some spell to keep out an evil spirit."

"Perhaps I am," he answered. "Tonight I will sleep in peace knowing that Lucy is safe."

We left that night, feeling confident and in much need of sleep.

September 13

I picked up Van Helsing at his hotel, and we went out to Hillingham. We were met by Mrs. Westenra.

"Doctors, you will be glad to know that Lucy is still well. I checked on her this morning but did not go in. She was still sleeping soundly."

"Aha, my treatment is working," Van Helsing said with a smile.

"Yes, but you can't take all the credit.

I checked on her in the night and found the room awfully stuffy. I took away all those strong-smelling flowers and opened the window. You will be pleased, I am sure."

As she moved off, Van Helsing and I darted up the stairs. We threw back Lucy's door and, as we suspected, found her white as a ghost. Quickly, we again got ready for a transfusion. This time, Van Helsing gave his blood, and I operated. Lucy awoke later in the day, not looking too bad considering what she had been through.

What can it all mean? Van Helsing is keeping his thoughts to himself. He plans to stay until Lucy has improved. He then must return to Amsterdam for a day. I will leave in the interim. I must attend to Renfield. I have just received a note from the asylum that he escaped again. Although he was caught and brought back, he attacked some workers carting off boxes from that old house next to the asylum. He is becoming much more violent than ever. It troubles me. What is it about that house next door?

September 18

I am just off the train, arriving once more at Hillingham. I received a telegram from Van Helsing one day late, requesting that I be with Lucy on the night of September 17. I fear what may have happened to her last night. I know how things turn around when she is left alone.

Chapter 10

THE WOLF

Note left by Lucy Westenra
September 17

I feel that I'm dying of weakness and barely have the strength to write. I am putting down what has happened so that no one will get into trouble. I was afraid to sleep all night, for Dr. Van Helsing and Dr. Seward were not here to watch over me. Mother came in at one point and lay down with me.

Suddenly, there was a howl and then

a crash at the window. A gray wolf had jumped into the room. Mother struggled to sit up and then fell over. I could feel her hands grow cold and knew she was gone. I tried to get up, but a swirl of glowing dust came through the window. I could not move and soon I lost consciousness.

When I awoke, I called to the maids. They covered mother, but they were so upset that I had to send them to have a glass of wine to calm their nerves. Just then the door opened and closed. They screamed, and I had to force them out of my room. Now I am finishing this statement. I can feel myself dying. Oh, Arthur!

Dr. Seward's Diary
September 18

When I arrived at Hillingham, I found that I could not get in. No one would come to the door, and all the windows were locked. Van Helsing walked up soon after I arrived. He was upset that I had not been with Lucy, but I explained about the telegram arriving late. We then decided to break into the house. What we found was too shocking!

All the maids were unconscious on the floor, having been drugged. Lucy was white as a ghost, and her mother was cold to the touch. Van Helsing motioned

that Mrs. Westenra was dead, but when he came to Lucy, his face lit up.

"All is not lost," he said. "Let's put her into the bath and get her blood flowing."

The hot bath seemed to revive her a little. After we got her back to her room and covered her, we went downstairs to talk of what should be done. To my surprise, my friend Quincey Morris was in the sitting room.

"I came at once," he said, "as soon as I got this telegram from Arthur, telling me how ill Lucy has been. What can I do?"

"A brave man's blood is all we need," Van Helsing answered.

We rushed Quincey up to Lucy's room and performed another blood transfusion. Much to our happiness, she got some color in her cheeks and her breathing eased.

I went downstairs with Quincey to revive the maids and get the poor fellow some food and drink. When I returned to

Lucy's room, I found Van Helsing reading a note. He handed it to me. It was from Lucy, but I could not understand its meaning.

"The wolf," I started. "Could it have been the one that escaped from the zoo last night? The story was in this morning's paper. Or is she mad?"

"Dear John, you will understand in time."

September 19

Lucy was in a state all night. She was afraid to sleep, but too weak to keep herself from sleeping. By morning, she was hardly able to turn her head and could not eat anything.

We had already telegraphed Arthur, and in the afternoon he arrived. He and Van Helsing are sitting up with her. It is now one o'clock in the morning. I will go relieve them soon.

September 20

I have not the heart to write, but I must. Poor Lucy grew worse during the day. Her gums were more drawn back, and her teeth seemed to grow long and sharp. Her breathing became more unsteady, and by nightfall she was dying. She called to Van Helsing, and he came to her side.

"My true friend," she said. "Guard my poor Arthur. Protect him from me, and give me peace."

"I will do all that," Van Helsing replied. "I promise you."

Once more Lucy's eyes met Arthur's, and then she died. Quincey and I took Arthur out of the room. When I returned, Van Helsing was looking at Lucy. A strange change had come over her. She was not more pale but more rosy. It was as though she were still alive, or as if death gave her life!

"Poor girl," I said. "There is peace for her at last."

"Not so," Van Helsing replied. "It is only the beginning, but for now we must wait and see. Look at this."

The professor pulled back Lucy's gown from her neck. The puncture wounds had healed!

Chapter

VAN HELSING'S MISSION

Dr. Seward's Diary
September 22

It is all over. Lucy and her mother were buried yesterday. Quincey has left with Arthur. That poor fellow. Just this morning Arthur received word that his father passed away in the night. I am afraid that it will all be too much for him. I have remained another day with the professor. He shall go to Amsterdam tonight, but shall return.

Van Helsing got permission from

Arthur to go through Lucy's papers. He has read her journal and letters and has become excited by evidence he has found. He wants to speak with one of Lucy's friends, someone who lives in Exeter. I suppose it has something to do with what he's found. But I'm not at all sure what is happening. The professor is being very mysterious.

Mina Harker's Diary
On the train from London
September 22

Oh, how happy I have been with Jonathan, and now more trouble. It seems like only yesterday since my last entry, but so much has happened in between. Jonathan and I returned to London and began to live with Mr. Hawkins, who thought of Jonathan as his own son. We were so happy for awhile. Jonathan's health improved, and he became a partner in the business. Now

Mr. Hawkins has died, and Jonathan has had another attack.

The attack occurred in London. We were walking along, when all of a sudden Jonathan grabbed my arm. His strength seemed to go out of him completely, and his face went white. He was looking at a tall man standing on the walk across the street.

"What's wrong?" I asked.

"It is the man himself," he replied.

I did not understand, but I stood there in silence watching Jonathan's face. It was a picture of terror. His eyes seemed to bulge out in fear.

"I believe it is the Count, but he has grown young," he said.

The man caught a cab, and we went on our way. However, Jonathan has remained in a state of shock. I think I must try to discover why he is so afraid. He has kept his diary wrapped like a parcel and has made me promise never to read it unless there is cause. I think the time and the cause have come.

Later

We have just arrived home from London and have found another piece of bad news. A telegram from a gentleman named Dr. Van Helsing informs us of Lucy's and Mrs. Westenra's death. How shall we ever bear all this sorrow!

September 25

Again, so much has happened since my last entry. I received a letter from Dr. Van Helsing, the professor who treated Lucy in her last days. He was in London, just back from Amsterdam and wanted to speak with me. I sent a telegram asking him to come today for lunch. Of course, he wants to speak of Lucy, but I hope that he can also help me with Jonathan's condition. Now that I've read Jonathan's journal, I am truly confused and afraid.

Later

The professor has come and gone. What a strange meeting! Dr. Van Helsing asked me for my diary. He wanted to read it because he felt that it would help him solve the mystery behind Lucy's death. I was not at all sure what he was looking for, but I was glad to be of help.

At the same time, I asked him to read Jonathan's diary. I told the professor that I was afraid, that the diary spoke of many

evil things, things that occurred while Jonathan was in Transylvania. Dr. Van Helsing listened very closely to all I had to say. He then took the journal and promised to read it very carefully. He will counsel me on what course to take with Jonathan.

September 26

Van Helsing sent a telegram last night. He had read my diary as well as Jonathan's. He assured me that Jonathan was not crazy. He also requested another interview, but with the both of us! So, I invited Dr. Van Helsing to breakfast, and he came this morning on the ten o'clock train. Jonathan seemed relieved to hear the professor assure him that what happened in Transylvania was real.

"Now, I have much to do," the professor said. "The task that lies before me is very great. I must ask you for your help. I would like to see all the papers you have that concern the Count."

Jonathan was only too happy to help Dr. Van Helsing. He and I both promised to do whatever we could to assist the professor. Now that Dr. Van Helsing has left for Carfax, where Dr. Seward lives, we anxiously await his call.

Dr. Seward's Diary
September 26

Truly, I am perplexed at the professor's behavior. He seems to have lost his mind. He arrived this afternoon by train and came into my office and threw the morning paper into my lap.

"Look at this!" he exclaimed. "What do you make of it?"

The article described how some young children had been led away from their homes at night. The morning after, the children had returned very weak, with puncture marks in their neck. When questioned, they said that a woman had taken them off. They did not remember how they got their wounds. The authorities were suggesting that the children had been bitten by bats.

"I do not know what to make of this, Professor," I said.

"Come now, John," he said. "The wounds are like those of poor Lucy."

"Are you suggesting, Professor, that Lucy was bitten by a bat?" I asked.

"No," he answered. "You must open your mind. You must begin to believe in things that you have not believed in as a man of science."

I thought hard and could find no possible answer. It was all too strange.

"Professor, you must again let me be your student, for I cannot come up with the answer to this mystery. I can only imagine that what bit these children is what bit Lucy."

"I am afraid it is much worse than that, John," he said. "The bites in the necks of the children were made *by* Lucy."

"Dr. Van Helsing!" I exclaimed. "That is absurd. Have you gone mad?"

"Oh, if only I were!" he answered. "But it is not my mind that has worked this evil. As I told you before, you must open your mind. Tonight we go to Lucy's tomb. There we will find the proof to all I say. Lucy has become one of the undead. She is a vampire!"

Chapter

LUCY'S TOMB

Dr. Seward's Diary
Continued

I must say that a feeling of gloom came over me when Van Helsing announced that we would spend an evening in the graveyard. Now, as I think over the night's events, I am full of fear. Never has my logic been more challenged. Never has my courage been more tested.

We went to the churchyard after nightfall. Van Helsing had a copy of the key to Lucy's tomb made for Arthur but had not given it to him yet. He used this key, and we entered the tomb. It felt gloomy inside, even after Van Helsing lit some candles he had brought. Then, when the professor began to take the screws out of Lucy's coffin, I felt a shiver go up my spine.

"Professor, what are you doing?" I asked.

"I plan to convince you that Lucy is a vampire," he replied.

He finished taking the screws out and moved the top aside. I stepped over, feeling

very uneasy, and looked inside. I couldn't believe it! The coffin was empty.

"What do you make of this, John?" he asked.

"I don't know," I answered. "Perhaps someone has stolen her body."

The professor sighed and put the lid back. He then gathered all his things and led me outside. After locking the door, he told me to go to one side of the churchyard. He would go to the other.

We stood for some time, watching out for . . . I knew not what. Then, something white seemed to move in the distance. It drew closer. It was a woman in a gown, holding a child. She headed toward Lucy's tomb. Van Helsing and I followed. Suddenly, we both came upon the child on the ground, left behind by the woman. The child was all right, except that it had two puncture marks on her neck.

"See here," Van Helsing exclaimed.

"This proves nothing," I said. I could not bear to think that what Van Helsing had said about Lucy was true.

"Come," he said. "We must leave the child near the night watchman, so that she will be found and we will not be suspected of having carried her off from her home."

We stood by until we saw that the child was discovered. We then hurried off, before we were found in the churchyard.

It is now very late, and I must get some sleep. Van Helsing plans to call on me at noon, so that we can return to the tomb. Why, I do not know.

September 27

We returned to the churchyard as planned. Once again, we entered Lucy's tomb. It was not as gloomy as it was the night before. I did not know why we were going, since we had already found the coffin empty. I was trying to be patient with the professor. I have learned to trust his thinking.

He began unscrewing the lid as he had before. After this task was finished, he motioned for me to come close. There, to my great surprise, was Lucy. She looked lovelier than ever. Her cheeks were still rosy, and her lips were as red as blood! The professor began to explain.

"Here is some form of life that is not well known by us. Lucy was bitten by a vampire, and now she is 'undead.' At night,

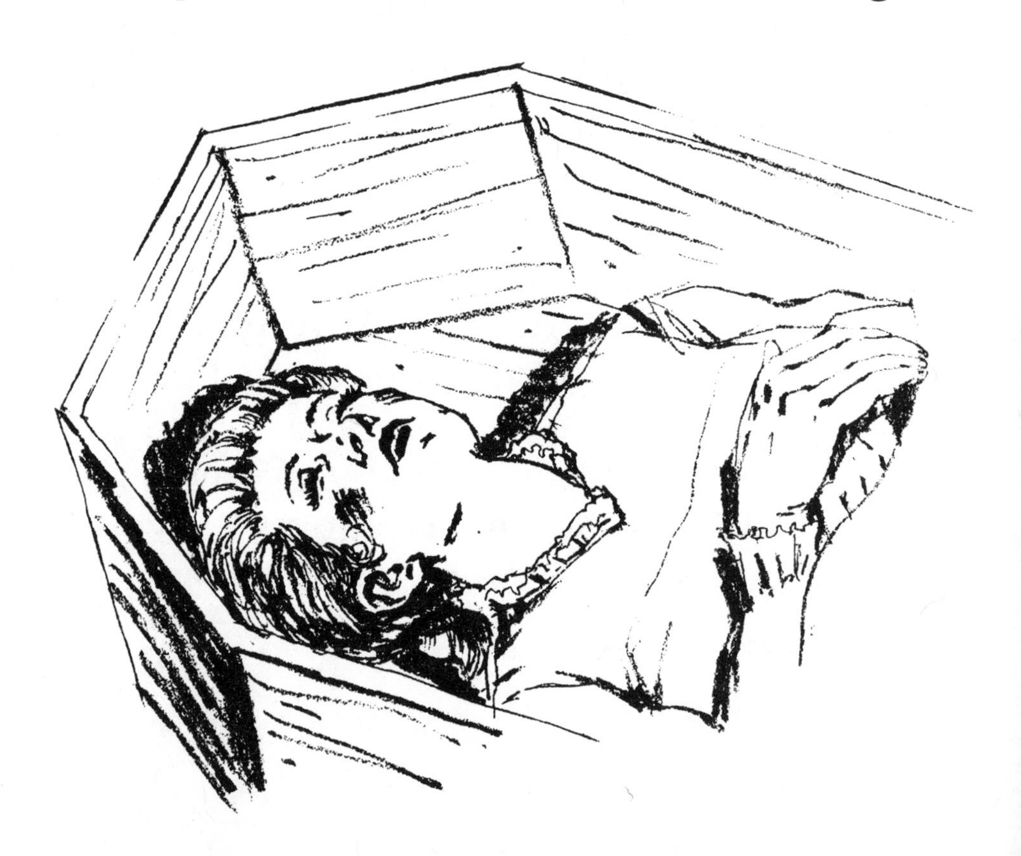

she must feed on the blood of the living, and during the day she must return to her home here in this tomb."

"What shall we do?" I asked.

"So!" he exclaimed. "You believe me now."

"Nothing else makes sense," I answered.

"Well, John," he said. "Today, we do nothing, for there are others we must convince. We must telegram Arthur and Quincey. They must see what we have seen. We will need their help when we go hunting for the vampire that bit Lucy. We shall return with them tomorrow night."

"How about these children who have been bitten?" I asked. "Will they become vampires?"

"No, for we shall destroy the vampire in Lucy. The children will not be bitten again and will forget what has happened."

I shuddered to think of the task that lay ahead. I had no idea what had to be done, but I guessed at how frightening it would be. The professor fixed the lid, and we left.

September 28

This afternoon, Arthur and Quincey arrived. They met us at Van Helsing's room at the hotel. They were very curious, but I could not give them any hint as to what was happening. I was still unsure of it all, that what I had seen was real. Also, I did not know what Van Helsing intended that night.

Poor Arthur and Quincey sat patiently, listening to the professor explain the bites on Lucy's neck, the disappearance of children, and our visit to the churchyard.

"You mean to say," Arthur started, "that you saw Lucy walking, that her coffin was empty and then it was not?"

"That is correct!" the professor said. "And now we plan to return tonight and give Lucy peace."

"How will you do that?" Quincey asked.

"We must drive a stake through her heart," Van Helsing answered.

Shocked, we all jumped out of our chairs.

"Surely, you must be out of your mind!" Arthur exclaimed.

"I only ask that you go with me," Van

Helsing answered calmly. "Once you see how things are, you may decide whether you are with me or against me."

We agreed to join him. The professor had already removed the garlic and crucifix left on our last visit. Lucy, or the thing that was once Lucy, was free to leave at nightfall. We waited until well after dark and went to her tomb. Again, it was empty. Arthur was in shock. We had to lead him out of the tomb.

Just as Van Helsing and I had done before, we waited in the churchyard for Lucy to return. We did not have to wait long. Soon we spotted a movement across the way. As the figure neared, we surrounded her and shined our lanterns. It was Lucy!

She broke through our ranks and fled to her tomb, slipping like smoke through the crack of the door. We followed, with Van Helsing leading the way. We found her in her coffin, with a drop of blood still on her lips. Arthur was unable to speak.

"Dear fellow," Van Helsing started. "Remember, this thing is not Lucy. We must free Lucy. We must do as I described, but shouldn't you be the one to give Lucy back her soul?"

"Yes," Arthur answered bravely. "Give me the stake."

The poor man held the stake high, then hammered it into Lucy's heart. The thing in the coffin at first squirmed and screeched like the demon that it was. Then, a peace came over it.

"You have done it, Arthur," Van Helsing said. "All is well with Lucy. Now we have other work to do. Two nights from now, we shall meet at John's, at the asylum in Carfax. Then we shall come up with a plan. Evil still lurks about us, and it is more powerful than what we have dealt with so far."

Part Four

HUNTING DOWN COUNT DRACULA

Chapter

GATHERING EVIDENCE

Dr. Seward's Diary
September 29

When we returned to Van Helsing's hotel, there was a telegram from Mrs. Mina Harker. It said she would be coming by train the next morning, which is today. Her husband was going to Whitby, and she was coming with important news.

"Ah, that good woman," said the professor. "She was a friend to poor Lucy and has had much to add to my knowledge. She will be of great help to us. I want you to read her journal, and her husband's as well. She has typed a duplicate of them so that I might read them, as the originals are in shorthand."

The professor handed me a stack of papers.

"Also, John," he continued, "you must meet her train, for I shall return to Amsterdam this morning. Take her to your asylum. I shall return soon."

I did as I was instructed. Mrs. Harker did not seem to mind the asylum too much, although she did shudder as we entered the door. We went to my study, where we talked for awhile.

"Jonathan and I have been hard at work," she said. "We have been putting our diaries together, so that all the events are in order. This way, it is easier to see how things have happened. I see you have been reading the copies I gave to the professor."

She looked toward the stack of papers on my desk.

"Yes, I too shall examine the evidence," I answered. "My own diary may be of some help."

I got up and took out my diary from the desk drawer.

"Then I shall read it, Dr. Seward," she said, "and I will add it to our own."

She went to her room, and I remained in my study. I read both of the Harkers' diaries as well as the deeds and other papers Mr. Harker had given to Van Helsing.

It's strange that it never occurred to me that the house next door might be the Count's hiding place. The Count! He must be a vile man, if he could be called a man. And Renfield! What has he to do with the Count?

When Mrs. Harker came to my study in the afternoon, having read my journal, she was interested in Renfield's case, too. She asked if she could see him. I took her to Renfield's room. He was as gentle as a

lamb and very polite to her. It seems he has two ways of behaving. I suspect that he is in his excited and violent state when the Count is near. We left Renfield and returned to our work.

Jonathan Harker arrived in the evening. He and his wife went back to their rooms to continue sorting through the evidence. Apparently, he has traced those dreadful boxes belonging to the Count. They arrived at Whitby on that strange Russian ship called the Demeter, which had come from Varna. The boxes

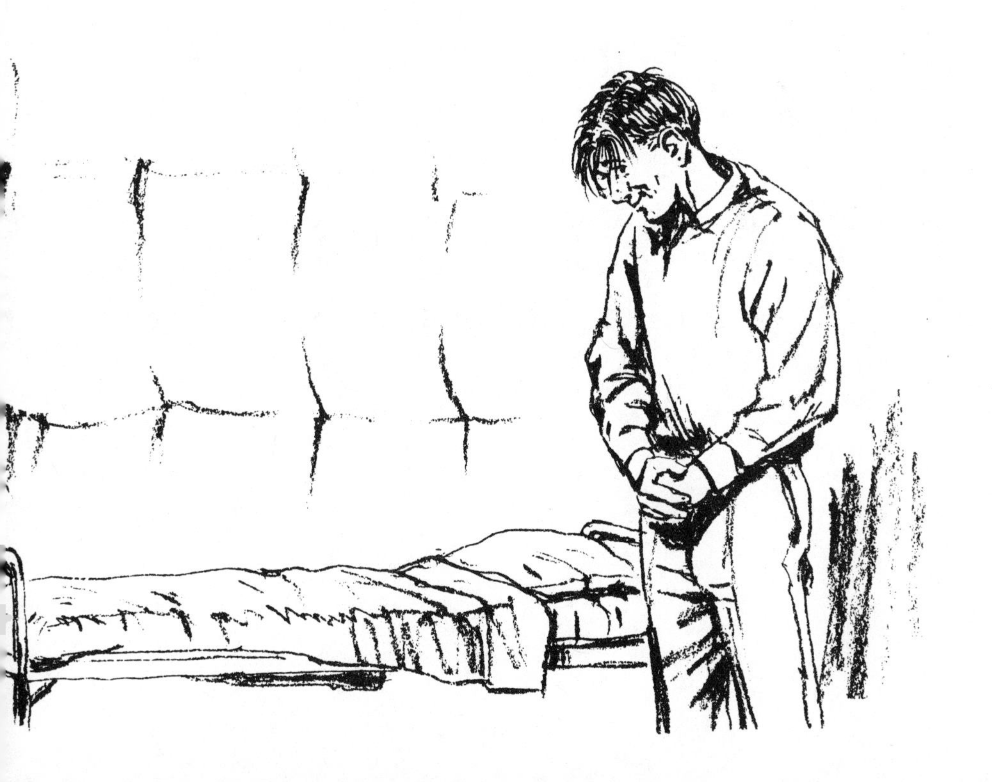

were claimed by a lawyer there and carried to the house next door, where they were placed in the old chapel. There were fifty in all. But, I recall that some were carted away by workmen. It was these very workmen that Renfield attacked that second time he escaped. Oh, it is a mystery!

September 30

I was out today until the late afternoon. After taking care of some business, I picked up Dr. Van Helsing at the train station. We then went to the asylum and found that Arthur and Quincey were there. They had already read the diaries and had spoken to Mrs. Harker. They were both quite taken with her intelligence and kindness. She is a comfort to us after having lost Lucy.

After dinner, we all met in my study. Dr. Van Helsing began by going over all the evidence. He described what Jonathan observed in the Count—how

the man was very strong, how he scaled the castle walls, how he slept in a coffin full of dirt, and so on. Van Helsing also explained to us that the Count could transform himself into other things. He had most likely turned himself into the great dog that had jumped from the *Demeter* when it hit shore at Whitby. He also had turned himself into a bat in order to get to Lucy.

Just then, Quincey jumped from his seat and left the room. A few minutes later we heard gunfire. The bullets hit the wall just outside the window, and one came in and hit the ceiling. Mrs. Harker jumped in fright. A moment later, Quincey was back in the room. He had seen a bat sitting at the window and had gone out to shoot it. He had missed, however. We all settled back down, and the professor began talking again.

"I have researched all that is known about vampires while in Amsterdam," Van Helsing continued. "We must keep in mind certain things regarding the Count, such as his strength and his ability to transform himself. His power does grow weaker at the coming of the day, and he can only transform himself at noon or at sunset. Also, he cannot enter anywhere unless there is someone in the household who invites him. Afterward, he may come as he pleases. So, in this asylum we are safe unless we ask him in. There are things that we can use to protect ourselves, such as the crucifix and garlic."

Van Helsing then began to talk about the boxes that the Count had brought from Transylvania. He explained that the Count had probably brought so many from his homeland because he needed to have many safe places to hide throughout London.

Vampires need to sleep on the earth of their homeland. They usually keep their boxes in places that were once holy, such as the old chapel next door. Our task is to find all these hiding places and destroy the boxes.

"According to John's diary," the professor continued, "six of the boxes have already been removed from the house next to the asylum. The Count may have moved others, too, or may be about to move them. We must go there tonight and see for ourselves."

The professor then armed each of us with a crucifix and strands of garlic. He told Mrs. Harker that she should go to bed. The Count's house would be a dangerous place.

Chapter

LOOKING FOR CLUES

Dr. Seward's Diary
October 1

Last night before we left for the Count's house, the attendant came to tell me that Renfield was demanding to see me. I went off to the patient's room and found him quite upset.

"Dr. Seward, you must release me at once," Renfield said. "I cannot tell you why. I am not allowed. But it is very important."

"I cannot release you, Renfield," I said.

"Well, then," he answered. "I will not be held responsible. It is in your hands. Later, perhaps, you will remember that I did try to convince you to take me from this house."

I could not understand what he meant by this. But now that I know he has something to do with the Count, I cannot let him leave so easily. I left immediately and joined Van Helsing, Harker, Arthur, and Quincey.

We climbed over the wall separating the asylum from the old house next door. Luckily, since Harker was the lawyer who found this house for the Count, he had a key. We opened the door and entered. I must say that it was then that I realized that my heart was pounding against my chest.

The whole place was thick with dust. There were footprints in the dust on the floor. On a table in the hall was a great bunch of keys with a label on each.

"Jonathan," the professor said, "you know this place better than we. Can you lead us to the chapel?"

"I will try," he whispered.

We made only a few wrong turns going to the chapel. When we came to its big wooden doors, the professor jiggled the key in the lock, and the door opened. Out came a foul odor that smelled like dirt and blood, or maybe evil itself.

After examining the boxes, we found that there were only twenty-nine left out

of the fifty. We would have to track down the other twenty-one somehow. The professor motioned for us to leave. We were somewhat puzzled, for we thought we had come to destroy the boxes. But we left, as he insisted.

When we got back to the asylum, Dr. Van Helsing explained that we could not let the Count know what our intentions were. We needed to find out where the other boxes were, then destroy all of them within the same day. Otherwise, the Count would have time to move them.

We all went to bed and overslept. Curiously, Mrs. Harker slept even later. Harker felt that she must have been upset last night by the dangerous mission we undertook. She did seem very tired when I saw her and complained of having bad dreams. We've decided not to tell her what we are doing. It will only upset her further.

Renfield, too, was in a state this morning. When I visited him, he was gloomy and quite sad. I must keep my eye on him.

At present, Harker, Quincey, and Arthur have gone out separately to follow up on clues as to the location of those other twenty-one boxes. Van Helsing is doing research. Mrs. Harker is in her room. I shall finish my round of work, and tonight we will all meet again.

Mina Harker's Diary
October 1

It is strange to be kept in the dark. They have all agreed to keep me out of their activities from now on. I suppose it is for the best. It is all so horrible. Last night, after they left, I went to bed but could not sleep. I was full of anxiety.

I cannot remember how I fell asleep. I remember hearing the sudden barking of dogs. I got up and looked out the window. All was dark and silent, except for a thin streak of white fog that crept across the yard and up the side of the house.

I got back in bed and heard some strange noises coming from Renfield's room. It sounded as if he were pleading with someone. Then there was the sound of a struggle. I imagined that the attendants were trying to calm him.

I must have fallen asleep soon after, for I began dreaming that the fog was pouring into the room through the cracks in the door. I could not move at all, and could see the fog become a pillar in the room. At the top of this pole of smoke were two red eyes. Before the dream was over, a white face came out of the fog and bent over me. I may as well have not slept at all, for I awoke totally exhausted.

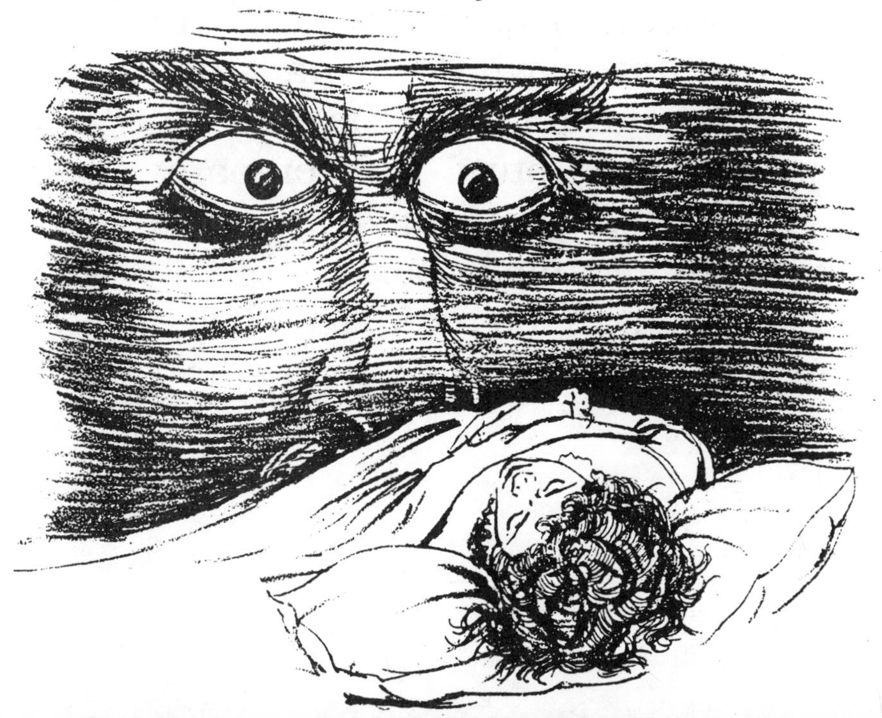

Dr. Seward's Diary
October 2

After dinner last night, when Mrs. Harker went off to bed, we all sat around and discussed what we had discovered that day. Harker was the only one with any news. He found the company of fellows who carried off those boxes from the Count's house next door.

Harker discovered that these men had taken a total of six boxes to a house at Mile End, another six to a house in Bermondsey, and nine to a house in Piccadilly. Harker visited the house in Piccadilly. He says it is very old and run down, but he could see no way to get into it.

"We shall break the door down," Arthur exclaimed.

"See here, Art," I said. "We cannot commit burglary in the middle of Piccadilly. There are plenty of people around."

"Right," Van Helsing said, "but we shall, and we shall do it in broad daylight."

We all looked to the professor. Was he out of his mind?

"It is simple, gentlemen," he continued. "Our Lord Arthur Godalming will hire a locksmith to come and open the door for him. No one will suspect such a fine gentleman of breaking and entering, especially if the crime is done in the middle of the day."

We could all see how clever this plan was and chuckled joyously.

I have just been told that Renfield has met with some accident. I shall go to him at once.

Chapter

ENCOUNTERS WITH THE COUNT

Dr. Seward's Diary
October 3

I must put down as accurately as I can all that has happened. It is all so horrible, but I shall try to stay calm.

When I got to Renfield's room, I found him lying on the floor in a pool of blood. He had received some terrible injuries. His head was bleeding and his face was greatly bruised. When I turned him, I found that his back was broken. Such an injury as this could not have

occurred simply by his falling out of bed.

Van Helsing arrived in the room with his surgical bag. We sent the attendant away, in case Renfield were to regain consciousness and say something regarding the Count. Just then Arthur and Quincey came in. As we were talking, Renfield took a great breath and awoke.

"Oh, Doctor," he said, "I've had a terrible dream. But it wasn't a dream really. I must tell you everything. The night I asked you to release me, I could not tell you. I felt that my tongue was tied. He came to my window. He promised me things, like rats and dogs and cats. I looked out my window, and there they were—thousands of these animals running across the yard.

"I found myself saying, 'Come in, Lord and Master!' He slid in through the window and left through my door, laughing at me. All day I waited for him to return. Then, tonight when he came, I thought of Mrs. Harker. It occurred to me that he had been sucking the life from her. I became angry and tried to hold him. I wanted to keep him from leaving my room, but he threw me to the floor and left. He is here, now."

Renfield closed his eyes, and his breathing became faint. He was dying. I called the attendant, and we left for the Harkers' room. When we came to the door, Van Helsing turned the knob but it was locked. I threw myself upon it, and it flew open. We all entered, and there before us was the Count!

He was standing, holding Mrs. Harker's head to his chest. Jonathan was in a deep sleep on the floor. The Count's eyes blazed red. His chest was bleeding, and on Mrs. Harker's lips was blood. As we stepped forward, holding our crucifixes toward the Count, he threw Mrs. Harker down and stepped backward. Suddenly, he evaporated into a thin vapor and left through the window.

Harker awoke then and cried out to his wife. She was in tears on the floor. Van Helsing pulled Mrs. Harker up from the floor and wrapped her in a blanket. We explained to them what had happened, how we knew the Count was in

their room. They were both very upset. Then, Mrs. Harker told us what she could remember of the Count.

"Jonathan was in a deep sleep and did not move at all. I was afraid and tried to wake him but couldn't," she said. "Suddenly, my body seemed very heavy. I felt that I was asleep, but I was aware of all that was happening. I saw a mist come in through the door, and there he was, standing above me. He leaned down and placed his cold lips on my neck. It felt as though all the life was being drawn out of me. Then he stood and pulled me off the bed.

"He said, 'And so you would play your brains against mine. You would help these men to hunt me. You will all discover what it means to cross my path. Now, you are flesh of my flesh, blood of my blood, kin of my kin. Later, you shall be my helper.' With that, he cut himself with his sharp nail and drew me to his chest, where the blood was running. Oh, it is too much for me to bear!"

The sun was now coming up in the eastern sky, and the room was becoming lighter. Harker was still and quiet, and we could see with the morning's light that his hair had turned from black to white!

Dr. Seward's Diary Continued

Although we were all anxious and worried, we went off to breakfast to discuss what we should now do. We all agreed that Mrs. Harker should be kept informed, not shut out from our plans. As usual, Van Helsing had thought everything out before we even finished our breakfast.

"It is well," he began, "that we did nothing to the boxes in the house next door. Had we destroyed them, the Count would have known our purpose and moved the other boxes from the houses in Piccadilly, Mile End, and Bermondsey. Today then, is ours. Until the sun sets tonight, the Count cannot melt into thin air or fly away as a bat. If he comes through a doorway, he must do so as a man would do.

"We will first destroy his boxes, for they are the places he goes to for safety. If we come upon him while doing this, we shall destroy him by driving a stake through his heart. First we shall go to his house next door. Then we shall all go to Piccadilly, gain entrance, and destroy the boxes there. Then Arthur and Quincey will find the houses in Mile End and Bermondsey. After destroying those boxes, they shall return to Piccadilly. We shall then wait there for the Count if he is not already destroyed. Also, we shall take any papers of his that we find, for they may provide other clues that will help us."

We agreed that the professor's plan made sense and that we had to act quickly.

"We cannot fail," he said. "If we do, then Madame Mina is doomed. She has drunk the blood of the vampire, and so will be a vampire when she dies. The only way to save her is to destroy Count Dracula."

We were all silent. Harker had tears in his eyes, but Mrs. Harker straightened.

Her courage seemed to strengthen us all. We bounded from the table and got ready for our mission.

Out in the yard, we climbed over the wall and headed for the Count's house. We entered as we had before. We found no papers, but all twenty-nine boxes were still there. The professor began opening the boxes, and then the rest of us followed his example. The Count was not there, which in some way greatly relieved us but also caused some distress. We had to destroy him before he destroyed Mrs. Harker!

The professor took out great bottles of holy water from his bag. He began pouring the water into the boxes, wetting down the earth there and making it sacred.

"No vampire can come near holy ground," the professor explained, "although for his home he chooses

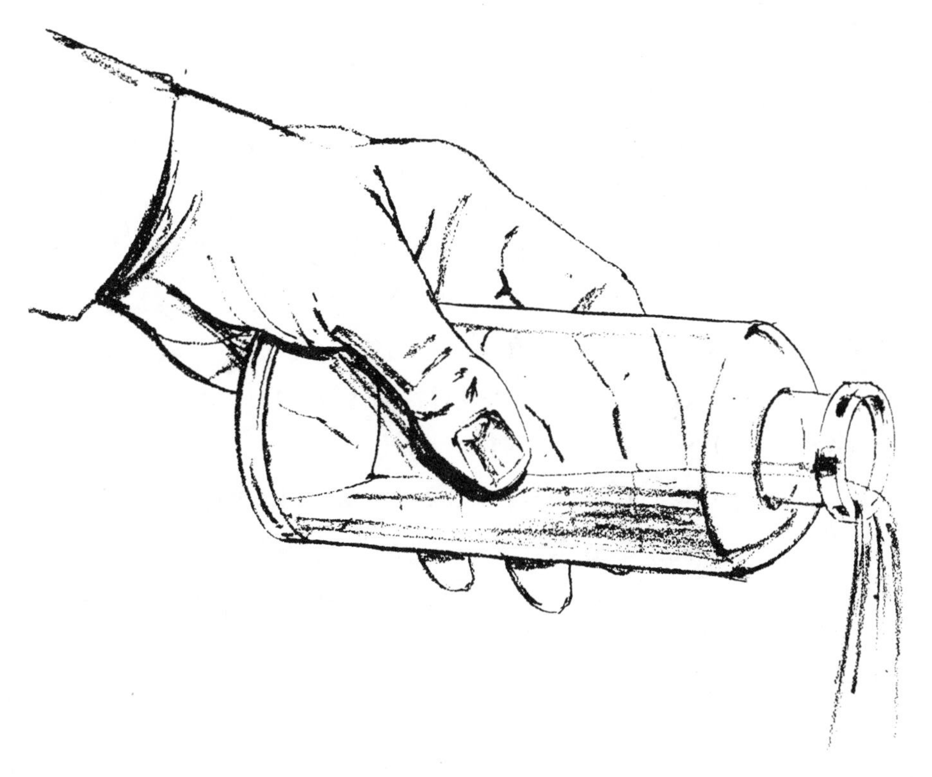

ground that was once holy. Now we make this place sacred again and close it off to the Count."

We left the place and headed for Piccadilly in great haste, for we had much to do.

As Jonathan had said, the house in Piccadilly was old and ruined and well guarded by public view. There was no way to gain entrance unless we broke a window or had a key to the door. We could not draw the law's attention, so we had to have a key.

According to our previous plan, Arthur paid a locksmith to make a key to the door. No one, including the police, suspected a thing. We entered and found the same foul smell that we had encountered in the house in Carfax. We began taking the lids off the boxes and wetting them with holy water. Much to our dismay, there were only eight boxes, not nine! Our work would not be done until we found that other box.

Arthur and Quincey set out for Mile

End and Bermondsey. While Harker, Van Helsing, and I waited, we went through all the papers we found there, studying them carefully for any clues that might lead to the other box.

Suddenly there was a knock at the door. We all jumped and looked at one another, then Van Helsing went to the door and opened it. There stood a telegraph boy. He handed in a message then went away. Van Helsing read the telegram aloud.

"Look out for D. He has just now, 12:45, come from Carfax hurriedly and hastens towards the south. He seems to be going round to all his houses and may be looking for you—Mina."

About half an hour later, another knock came at the hall door. Once again, we all jumped out of our seats. We all moved to the door with our crucifixes in hand, and Van Helsing threw back the door. It was only Arthur and Quincey. They came in quickly and closed the door.

"It is all right," Arthur said. "We found both places, and destroyed all twelve boxes."

"There is nothing left to do now but wait here for the Count," Van Helsing said. "But if he does not show up by five o'clock, we should return to Carfax. Madame Mina should not be left alone. Hush, there is someone coming."

We all got ready with our crucifixes, but before we knew what was happening, the Count had sprung into the room like a panther. Harker threw himself in front of the door. A horrible snarl came over the Count's face. Then Harker leapt toward him with a knife. The Count moved quickly, and only his coat was torn by the blade, but a bundle of money fell out from his coat to the floor.

All of us closed in on him, each with a crucifix in hand. He growled as an animal would, trapped by its hunters. Then, all of a sudden, he grabbed up some money from the floor and dashed under

Harker's arm. He jumped out the window and disappeared into the night.

"Ah," the professor said, "he fears us. But for now our work is done. We must go back quickly to Madame Mina, for she is not out of danger. Count Dracula has only one box left, and tomorrow we must start anew and find this last hiding place."

Chapter

THE FINAL STRUGGLE

Dr. Seward's Diary
October 4

Last night, Van Helsing fixed Mrs. Harker's room with garlic. He assured her that she could sleep in peace. We all took turns standing guard.

Just before dawn, Harker awoke the professor and the rest of us. Mrs. Harker wanted Van Helsing to hypnotize her. We all went to her room to listen to what she had to say.

"Hypnotize me, for I feel that then I

may speak about the Count," she said. "But you must do it before the dawn."

The professor did as Mrs. Harker requested. She seemed to go into a trance. There was a far-away look in her eyes.

"Where are you?" Van Helsing asked.

"I do not know. It is strange to me. I can hear water," she answered.

"Are you on a ship?" he asked.

"Yes. The men are stamping overhead getting ready to sail," she said.

The sun was now coming up in the sky, and we were all in the full light of day. Mrs. Harker sat up and looked around at us. She did not remember anything.

"The Count means to escape," Van

Helsing explained. "That is why in Piccadilly he grabbed the money from the floor. He knows with one box left and us after him that he is in danger. He is returning to Transylvania, and probably by the same route by which he came. Let us go to Whitby to find out. If it be true, we shall follow him to Transylvania."

Later

We have just found out that the Count has set sail on a ship called the *Czarina Catherine*, which is headed to Varna. It will take about three weeks to reach that port. We can make it there more quickly if we go by train. So, without losing time, we will first rest and then get ready for the journey. We'll take a ferry across the Channel, a train to Paris, and then travel by Orient Express to Varna.

Mrs. Harker has insisted on coming. She thinks that she can be of great help. The professor will continue to hypnotize her, so that we will know the whereabouts of the Count. The professor and I have spoken on this point. We both fear that she may come under the influence of the Count as we near his homeland. We must watch out for this.

October 15

We have arrived in Varna. There has been no news of the *Czarina Catherine*. Every day before sunrise and sunset, the professor hypnotizes Mrs. Harker. So far, she has only described the lapping of waves and the sounds of the men on board stomping overhead.

For now, we can only wait until the ship comes into port.

October 28

We have just found out from the shipping company that the *Czarina Catherine* got off course and entered the port of Galatz today at one o'clock. We cannot get a train going there until tomorrow, so we will wait.

It is evident to me and to the professor that the Count has been allowing Mrs. Harker to enter his mind during hypnosis so that he may enter hers. In this way, he has found out that we were in Varna awaiting his arrival. Still, we shall continue to hypnotize her.

October 30

We arrived in Galatz this morning, only to find that the ship has unloaded. The box was picked up by a man named Petrof Skinsky, who is known to deal with the Slovak people who run boats down the rivers. We set off to find Skinsky but were told that he had been found this very morning with his throat torn open, as if he had been attacked by a wolf! We

returned to the hotel where we had left Mrs. Harker. She could see right away that we had been unsuccessful. There was nothing we could do for the moment, so we all went to our rooms to get some rest.

Mina Harker's Diary
October 30

The men have returned to the hotel with sad hearts. They looked completely defeated when I first saw them. They have now gone off to sleep, and I am trying to think things through. I am sure I can figure out the Count's reasoning, what path he would take to get home.

In my trance this morning, after the professor had hypnotized me, I said something about hearing cows and water swirling near my ears. I think that the Count decided in London to get back to his castle by water. It is the most safe and secret way.

Once Skinsky claimed the box at

sunrise, and the Count was safely on land, the Count was able to appear from the box in his human form. Then, once Skinsky arranged for the box to be taken up the river, the Count killed Skinsky to wipe out any trace of his escape from us. The Count then returned to his box.

Now, I have only to determine which river he is on. Looking at the map, I can see that there are two rivers he could have taken. The Pruth looks easier for traveling. But the Sereth is joined by the Bistritza, which runs up round the Borgo Pass. This is where Jonathan's coach met the coach of the Count. It must be the Sereth he is on! I shall go wake the others.

Dr. Seward's Diary
Continued

Joy of joys! We are all so much happier now. Mrs. Harker's reasoning is brilliant and will surely lead us to the Count.

We will separate and approach the Count in different ways, on different paths. Quincey and I are going by land on horses. Dr. Van Helsing and Mrs. Harker are taking a coach, which the professor will be driving. They will go on the same road Harker traveled last spring. Harker and Arthur are driving a steamer up the river, in hot pursuit of the Count.

Having got the provisions we all need for our journey, and having brought weapons with us from England secretly, we are now setting out. I pray all goes well.

Dr. Van Helsing's Memorandum
November 5

After many days of traveling with little sleep, seeing strange things in the night, I have almost thought that I have gone mad. Our horses were killed during the night, I think by those women vampires from the castle. Luckily, I had thought to draw a circle around us and make it holy with the bread of communion.

With today's morning light, I recovered my strength and my nerve. I could see Castle Dracula up ahead. There was nothing to do but face its horrors.

I left Madame Mina asleep in the circle, and headed to the castle. It was a great work, this castle, but I had brought tools to do all I needed to do. I broke the door off its hinges and entered, then began looking for the three graves of the women and that of Count Dracula.

When I found them, I took off the lids one at a time. As we had to do with poor

Lucy, I destroyed these vampires. It was a horrible sight. They squirmed and squealed, then turned to dust as soon as the stake was in their heart.

These vampires out of the way, I opened the massive tomb that read "DRACULA." This was the home of the king vampire. With great pleasure, I wet the earth within this large box with holy water. He could never enter it again. Then I fixed the entrances, each with a crucifix.

This task was done, and I had to get back to Madame Mina. So, I hurried out into the fresh light of day. She was awake and waiting impatiently.

"Hurry," she said. "I know my husband is approaching. We must go to him."

We hurried off, but soon it began to snow. It seemed a blizzard was coming on. We took refuge in a cave, covering ourselves with our blankets.

After awhile, I heard the cracking of whips and the shouts of men. I got up and looked down the hill with my field-glasses. A wagon was heading up the hill. There were several gypsies guarding it, but none had guns. Inside the wagon was the box! And further down the hill, following closely, were Quincey and John.

"Look! Madame Mina, look! Look!" I called.

Madame Mina came to my side and took the spyglasses. Looking around some more, she spotted Jonathan and Arthur coming from the north.

"The gypsies are racing for the sun, and it is going down quickly," I said.

"Soon they will be upon us. Let's take cover and get out our weapons."

We crouched behind the rocks at the front of the cave, holding our guns ready. Closer and closer the gypsies drew to us. Suddenly we heard a shout go up.

"Halt!" screamed Jonathan.

Jonathan and Arthur dashed up to the wagon on one side, and John and Quincey on the other. They raised their pistols, and the gypsies stopped. Our men got down and tried to break through the gypsies. Jonathan managed to get on top of the wagon and, with great strength, throw the box to the ground.

The gypsies were now fighting our men. I could see the flashing of knives but heard no gunshot. Then I saw Quincey grab his side. Blood spurted onto the snow, and poor Quincey fell.

Just then, the sun began sinking below the mountain tops. The gypsies stopped fighting and pointed to the fading light. Jonathan took this chance and threw open the lid of the box. The gypsies fell back in horror. They turned and ran off down the hill.

Their fear did not affect our men. Jonathan reached into the box with his knife and, with all his might, sliced through Count Dracula's throat. At the same time, Arthur stabbed the Count in the heart. The box shook as the Count squirmed under the blades. It was a horror to see, but it left us all feeling greatly relieved.

By the time Madame Mina and I got to the wagon, the Count was a pile of dust and poor Quincey was dying. When he saw Madame Mina, though, a smile passed over his lips.

"I am only too happy to die now, seeing that your soul is safe," he said to her.

To our grief, he died then, and we were left to find our way back on that long journey to the beauty and peace of fair England.

ABOUT THE AUTHOR

BRAM STOKER was born on November 8, 1847 in Dublin, Ireland. A sickly child, Bram Stoker was kept company by his mother, who entertained him with tales of horror. His fascination with these tales later led him to write *Dracula*.

At Trinity College, Stoker became a champion track athlete and an honor student. After college, he took a civil service job in 1870, but then found creative work as a drama critic for the *Dublin Mail*.

In 1876, Stoker met Henry Irving and became his manager. While working tirelessly for Irving, Stoker found time to write and earn a law degree. In all, Stoker wrote seventeen books, but critics still agree that *Dracula*, published in 1897, is his greatest achievement. Stoker died in 1912.

The Young Collector's Illustrated Classics

Adventures of Robin Hood
Black Beauty
Call of the Wild
Dracula
Frankenstein
Heidi
Little Women
Moby Dick
Oliver Twist
Peter Pan
The Prince and the Pauper
The Secret Garden
Swiss Family Robinson
Treasure Island
20,000 Leagues Under the Sea
White Fang